A PARRAGON BOOK
Published by Parragon Books, Unit 13-17 Avonbridge Trading Estate,
Atlantic Road, Avonmouth, Bristol BS11 9QD
Produced by The Templar Company plc, Pippbrook Mill,
London Road, Dorking, Surrey RH4 1JE
Copyright © 1994 Parragon Book Service Limited
Designed by Janie Louise Hunt
Edited by Caroline Steeden
Printed and bound in Italy
ISBN 1-85813-663-6

THE FIRST BOOK OF

King Arthur

RETOLD BY CAROLINE STEEDEN
ILLUSTRATED BY TONY MORRIS

‖ •PARRAGON• ‖

This Book Belongs to

_____

_____

CONTENTS

THE SWORD IN THE STONE

Many years ago, there lived a great and noble king named Uther Pendragon. He ruled Britain wisely and brought peace to the land, after many years of war and suffering. He was helped by an adviser called Merlin the Enchanter, who made powerful magic.

Uther married a beautiful widow, called Igraine, who already had three daughters. After some time Igraine gave birth to the king's son. But sadly the baby had no time to bring his parents happiness, as soon after he was born, Merlin came to the king with terrible news.

"King Uther," said Merlin, "as you know, I can see into the future. Very soon you will become ill with a fever and you will die. It will be a terrible time and there will be great wars in Britain. Your son will be in danger, as many of your enemies will want to kill him. You must let me take him away to a secret place where he can live safely until he becomes a grown man."

Uther and Igraine were filled with sadness, but they trusted Merlin, and knew what he told them would come true. "You must take our child to safety," said King Uther. "No harm must come to him, for he has the best hope of bringing peace to Britain once more in the future."

So, one dark night, Merlin took the baby down a secret path and through the forest. He took him far away to the castle of a good knight called Sir Hector, who promised to take care of him, as if he were his own son. Merlin told Sir Hector to name the baby Arthur.

Soon afterwards the king fell into a fever and died, just as Merlin had said he would. The next eighteen years were terrible. There were many wars, and castles and villages were burned and destroyed. The people needed a strong ruler to bring peace to the land once more.

Merlin decided the time had come to reveal the secret he had kept for the last eighteen years. He went to London with a message for the Archbishop of Canterbury. Lords, ladies and peasants from all over the land came to hear what he had to say.

"I have great news," said Merlin. "This land will soon have a new king who will be even wiser and nobler than Uther Pendragon. The new king will bring peace and order to this land troubled by war and hunger."

Merlin told the Archbishop to gather all the knights of the realm in his cathedral on Christmas day for a special service.

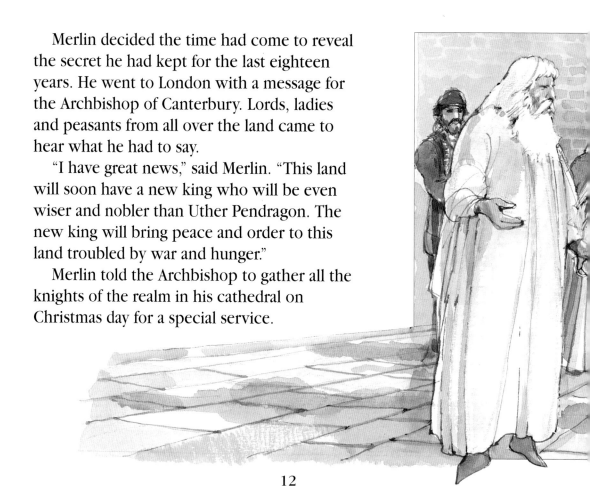

13

When they arrived at the cathedral, the knights found a marble rock outside, with a shining sword buried deep within it. They were astonished, and crowded around to see the wonderful sword, which had a golden handle set with precious jewels. A message was written at the bottom of the rock:

The knights that were gathered there all tried to pull the sword from the stone. They huffed and puffed and pulled with all their might, but no one could budge the sword an inch!

The Archbishop decided to send messengers across the land announcing a tournament on New Year's Day, when all could try to draw the sword from the stone.

16

On the day of the tournament, knights came from far and wide. Amongst them was Sir Hector with his son Sir Kay and his adopted son, Arthur, who by now was eighteen years old. There was to be much swordplay and jousting that day, and on the way there, Sir Kay realised he had left his sword at home. Sir Arthur rode back to fetch it, but found the gates locked, and no one home. He remembered passing a churchyard where he had seen a sword stuck in a stone, and, not wanting to disappoint his brother, rode quickly to the churchyard and with little effort pulled the sword smoothly from the stone. Arthur had not heard the stories of the sword, and was unaware of the importance of his actions.

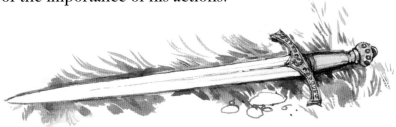

Sir Kay recognised the sword at once, and handed it to his father, saying, "Father, here is the sword from the stone. I must be the rightful king of Britain!"

Sir Hector looked doubtfully at his son and asked if he could swear truthfully that he had removed the sword himself. Sir Kay could not do so, and told his father that Arthur had given it to him.

"Where did you get it from, Arthur?" asked his father.

"I pulled it from the stone in the churchyard," replied Arthur.

Sir Hector rode back to the churchyard with his sons, and all of the other knights. They watched in amazement as Arthur replaced the sword, and then, the other knights having tried and failed once more to remove it, he stepped forward and swiftly slid the sword from the stone. The sword shone brightly as Arthur held it high in his right hand. Britain had a new king!

THE
ROUND TABLE

There came a time when King Arthur decided he should marry. He asked his good friend Merlin the Enchanter for his advice.

Merlin agreed it was time for him to marry, saying a man in his position should have a wife, and the kingdom needed a queen. He asked King Arthur whether there was any lady that he loved. Arthur told him that he loved the lady Guinevere, daughter of King Leodegrance of Camelard, who owned the Round Table. The table was given to him by Uther Pendragon, King Arthur's father.

21

"Guinevere is the most kind and beautiful lady in the world," said Arthur. He asked Merlin to go to King Leodegrance and tell him of his wish to marry Guinevere.

King Leodegrance was delighted. "This is the best news I have heard in ages," he said. "I am proud that such a noble and brave king as King Arthur wishes to marry my daughter. I will send him a gift to show him how pleased I am — the great Round Table given to me by his father, Uther, which has space enough for one hundred and fifty knights.

23

And so Merlin returned to King Arthur's
castle at Camelot with Guinevere, the
Round Table, and one hundred knights
sent by Leodegrance to serve Arthur
and take their place at the
Round Table.

King Arthur was overjoyed and made arrangements for the wedding to take place as soon as possible. He also asked Merlin to choose fifty worthy knights to fill the remaining seats at the Round Table. In a short time, Merlin had gathered forty-six of the bravest and most noble knights in the kingdom at King Arthur's court.

The wedding day soon arrived, and the Archbishop of Canterbury went to Camelot to marry King Arthur and Lady Guinevere at St Stephen's church. All the people of the kingdom were invited to join the celebration, and at the end of the solemn service the people cheered as the bells rang out over Camelot.

After the wedding service, Arthur asked the Archbishop to join them at court and bless each seat at the Round Table. A knight took each seat as it was blessed, until all the places were filled except for four.

Arthur and Guinevere took their places at the high table and Merlin asked the knights to stand and bow to their King and Queen. As the knights did so, gold letters mysteriously appeared on each chair, spelling the name of the knight who sat there. The knights gasped in amazement when they saw what had happened.

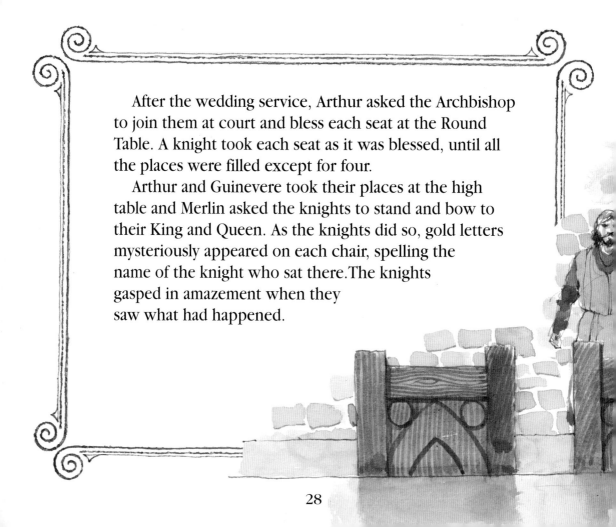

"Let me explain the wonders of the Round Table," said Merlin. "At this table all men are equal — no one sits at the head or the foot. When a knight is killed in battle, a new knight will take his place, and his name will also be written on his chair. The names of all the knights who sit at King Arthur's table will live on forever."

"But what about the empty seats?" asked King Arthur.

"One place is for the Black Knight," said Merlin. "You will soon hear tales of him and will face him in combat before he takes his place at this table. Two more are for brave knights who have yet to arrive, and the one left is the Perilous Seat. That seat must not be taken by any man except for the one for whom it is intended— and he is the best knight of them all."

Merlin looked so solemn, that no one, not even King Arthur, dared to ask who the best knight was.

Then King Arthur spoke to his knights as they sat at the table. "You must promise never to act unfairly and always to show mercy to those who ask for it. You must behave well towards women, and not fight without good reason or to gain possessions. If you break your promise, you will lose your place at the Round Table."

The knights all made this promise and agreed to renew it every year at the same time.

33

EXCALIBUR

Soon after the new King Arthur had set up his court at Camelot, he heard tales of a fearsome knight who was living in the forest nearby. He was the one known as the Black Knight, and was one of the strongest men in the land. He had been challenging knights as they passed through the forest and had defeated them all in battle — some had even been killed!

King Arthur decided to seek justice for the knights of his court, so he put on his armour and rode into the forest. He took Merlin with him who was the wisest enchanter in all the land.

They came to a clearing in the forest where the Black Knight had hung a shield from a tree. It had a warning written on it: "Whoever passes this way does so at his peril."

King Arthur struck the shield so hard that it rang out like thunder. The Black Knight appeared, dressed head to foot in black armour, and riding a black horse. "Why do you block the path of honest travellers through the forest?" asked King Arthur.

"I do as I please," said the Black Knight. "If you wish to pass you must fight me first."

"I will do just that," said King Arthur, "for the sake of all the knights you have defeated before."

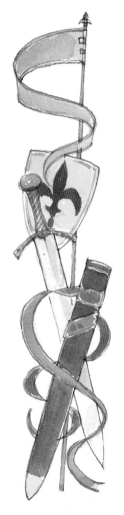

The two men turned around, then rode towards each other at an incredible speed. As they collided their lances broke in two, and they were both thrown to the ground. They drew out their swords and continued to fight. The battle went on for a long time, until Arthur struck the Black Knight's sword so fiercely that his own sword broke in two! Seeing King Arthur defenceless, and about to be overcome

by the Black Knight, Merlin decided it was time to take action! He put a spell on the Black Knight, who instantly fell into a deep sleep.

"What have you done, Merlin?" asked the king. "Have you killed the Black Knight with your magic?"

"He is only sleeping, my lord," said Merlin. "The kingdom should not lose its king in a battle like this. Come with me."

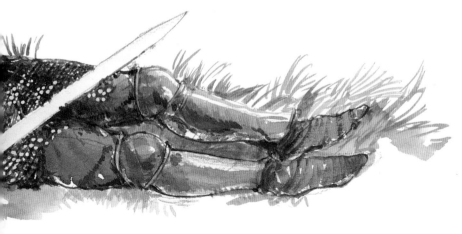

Merlin took Arthur to visit an old man who lived deep in the forest. The old man knew of secret potions, which he used to heal Arthur's wounds from the battle. Arthur was worried that he no longer had a sword to defend himself with, but Merlin told him not to worry. "Soon you will have a sword unlike any other," he said.

Merlin was able to make powerful magic, but he knew there were fairies who could make even stronger magic than his own, and he was taking Arthur to seek their help. Soon, they arrived at the edge of a shimmering blue lake. Arthur did not understand why Merlin had brought him here and thought it very strange.

41

As Arthur stood gazing out across the lake, he suddenly saw an incredible sight. Rising out of the middle of the lake was an arm draped in smooth, white silk, holding a gleaming sword.

"That is Excalibur," said Merlin, "the sword that I told you about. The Lady of the Lake will give it to you."

As they watched a beautiful lady rose out of the lake and walked across the water towards them. Her hair was as red as fire, and her blue eyes sparkled like the glittering lake.

43

"The Lady of the Lake lives beneath the water in a beautiful palace. She will tell you how to reach the sword," said Merlin.

The lady approached and bowed low before King Arthur.

"I am the Lady of the Lake. I have guarded your sword, Excalibur, for many years. This boat will carry you to the centre of the lake where you may claim the sword."

Seeing a boat gliding across the lake towards him, Arthur stepped into it as it reached the shore, and it at once turned and sailed to the centre of the lake. Arthur reached out and took the sword, and the outstretched arm slipped slowly back into the water. The boat turned once more, and took Arthur back to the shore where the beautiful Lady of the Lake had stood. But she too had vanished. Arthur leapt from the boat and showed Merlin the sword.

"Which do you like best?" asked Merlin. "The sword or the scabbard that holds it?"

"I like the sword, of course," said King Arthur.

"That is not a wise choice," said Merlin. "The scabbard is worth ten of the swords, for while you are wearing it, you will never lose a drop of blood. Be sure to keep it with you always."

Arthur assured his friend that he would. Then he turned on his horse, and galloped back to where he had left the Black Knight, who awoke at once, and the battle began again. Now that Arthur had Excalibur though, he soon won the fight.

The Black Knight fell to his knees in front of the king and asked him to spare his life. King Arthur agreed to spare him, and as he had fought so bravely, he offered to welcome him and his sons to the court at Camelot. King Arthur and the Black Knight made their peace, and the Black Knight and his sons served the King well, becoming some of the bravest knights in the land.

SIR LANCELOT
OF THE LAKE

There came a time for Merlin to fulfil his destiny and leave Camelot. Sadly he said farewell to Arthur, leaving him to rule alone as king, without the wisdom of his truest friend. It was time for Merlin to sleep his long sleep, until the day comes when he will wake once more. Slowly Merlin walked away from the court at Camelot and out into the night, where the Lady Nimue, Mistress of the Isle of Avalon, was waiting for him. She led him on a long journey, until at last they reached the court of Elaine, who was the queen of North Wales. There he asked to see

Elaine's son Lancelot of the Lake, so called because the Lady of the Lake took him when he was a baby and kept him hidden in her underwater realm for many years, following the death of his father King Ban.

Merlin made Lancelot promise to ride to Camelot for the next festival and tournament of jousting, and to tell King Arthur that it was Merlin's last wish that he should make Lancelot a knight at his table.

Merlin then slipped away into the night once more, and it is said that the Lady Nimue took him to a cave beneath her lake, where he fell into an eternal sleep from which he will only wake when Britain is in mortal danger.

And so it came to pass that in the middle of the next Royal Tournament at Camelot, a mysterious stranger appeared in their midst. King Arthur and Queen Guinevere were watching the jousting from the royal stand, and their curiosity was aroused by this unknown rider. His armour gleamed in the sunlight, but his visor was down and covered his face, and as he wore no colours or emblems to identify himself, he remained shrouded in mystery.

53

King Arthur welcomed him to the tournament and asked him to reveal his true identity, telling him that no knight should be ashamed of his name. But the stranger replied that he would first like to fight the bravest knights in Arthur's court, and only then, having proved his worth, would he reveal his name. Queen Guinevere was greatly impressed by this solemn and sincere knight, and asked Arthur if he might fight as her champion, since Arthur himself was unable to do so. King Arthur loved Guinevere dearly and was happy to agree to anything she wished, and so he gave the knight his blessing, and instructed him to fight well, for the royal honour was at stake. In his heart, Lancelot, overwhelmed by Guinevere's beauty, vowed then and there never to serve any other lady but her. This was to be the cause of his downfall later on, but that is another story altogether.

Out on the field, Sir Kay was the first to face him, determined to show the strange knight was unworthy of such royal attention. "Here is your chance to prove yourself, Knight with no name," he taunted. "Let's see what you are worth!"

Taking up their lances, the two knights rushed at each other, their horses' hooves thundering across the field. Skillfully, the unnamed knight swerved out off the way as Sir Kay's lance came swiping towards him, and momentarily caught off balance, Sir Kay went tumbling to the ground.

Dusting himself off, Sir Kay disappeared scowling into the crowd. One by one, the best knights at King Arthur's court took their turn up against him, and one by one all were thrown to the floor in defeat. At last the new champion turned to face King Arthur.

"You have defended my lady's honour well, brave knight, " said King Arthur. "Now it is time for you to reveal your true identity to our court."

Removing his helmet, the unnamed knight bowed low before the king. "I am Lancelot of the Lake, King Ban of Benwick's son," he said. "Merlin visited me on the way to his eternal resting place, and sent me here to be knighted and serve at your court. I was raised from a baby by the Lady of the Lake, who taught me many things, setting me challenges of skill and intellect which would seem almost impossible to solve. She taught me to be courageous, and worthy of a place at your table."

King Arthur smiled, overjoyed to have a knight sent by Merlin. Drawing Excalibur from its sheath, he gently touched Lancelot on each shoulder. "Arise, Sir Lancelot, it is a joy to welcome such a worthy warrior to Camelot."

That evening, Sir Lancelot took his place at the Round Table. His name had appeared on an empty chair beside that which was known as the Perilous Seat. That seat would only ever be taken by one knight, and that would be much later, at the time for the Quest for the Holy Grail.

Sir Lancelot became known as the bravest and most fearless knight, and had the greatest reputation of any knight at court. He was strong, chivalrous and noble, and his deeds brought glory to Camelot. King Arthur ruled wisely, fulfilling Merlin's prophecy. According to legend, he was the greatest king the world has ever known.